HENRY

JAMES

PERCY

TITLES AVAILABLE IN BUZZ BOOKS

First published 1990 by Buzz Books,
an imprint of the Octopus Publishing Group,
Michelin House, 81 Fulham Road, London SW3 6RB

LONDON MELBOURNE AUCKLAND

Copyright © William Heinemann Ltd 1990

All publishing rights: William Heinemann Ltd. All television
and merchandising rights licensed by William Heinemann Ltd
to Britt Allcroft (Thomas) Ltd exclusively, worldwide.

Photographs © Britt Allcroft (Thomas) Ltd 1985, 1986
Photographs by David Mitton, Kenny McArthur and
Terry Permane for Britt Allcroft's production of
Thomas the Tank Engine and Friends.

ISBN 1 85591 004 7

Printed and bound in the UK

EDWARD, GORDON AND HENRY

buzz books

Gordon, the Big Engine, always pulls the express. He is very proud of being the only engine strong enough to do so.

One day Gordon left the station with the express as usual. It was full of important

people, like the Fat Controller, and Gordon
was seeing just how fast he could go.

"Hurry! Hurry!" he said.

"Trickety-trock, trickety-trock,
trickety-trock," said the coaches.

Gordon went very fast and soon he could see the tunnel where Henry stood, bricked up and lonely.

Henry had been very foolish. He had gone into the tunnel and wouldn't come out again because he was afraid that the rain would spoil his lovely green paint.

The guard had blown his whistle; the fireman and passengers had argued with him; the men had pulled and pushed him but still Henry would not move.

Then, at last, they had given up. The Fat
Controller had ordered the men to take up
the old rails and to build a wall in front of
Henry. The other engines had to use the
tunnel at the other side.

Now Henry wondered if he would ever
pull trains again.

"Oh dear! Will the Fat Controller ever forgive me and let me out?" he said to himself that day, as he watched Gordon getting closer and closer to the tunnel.

"In a minute," Gordon said, "I'm going to poop-poop at Henry and rush through the tunnel and out again into the open!"

He was almost there when, crack,

"WHEE————EESHSHSH!"

And suddenly, there he was, going slower
and slower in a cloud of steam. His driver
stopped the train.

"What has happened to me?" asked
Gordon. "I feel so weak."

"You've burst a safety valve," said the
driver. "You can't pull the train any more."

13

"Oh dear," said Gordon. "We were going so nicely, too. And look, there's Henry laughing at me!"

All the passengers climbed out of the coaches and came to see Gordon.

"Humph!" said the Fat Controller.

"I never liked these big engines – always going wrong. Send for another engine at once."

They uncoupled Gordon. He had just enough puff to slink slowly into the siding, out of the way.

The guard went back to the yard to fetch another engine.

There was only Edward left in the shed.

"Gordon has burst a safety valve. Can
you help?" asked the guard.

"I'll come and try," said Edward.

17

When Edward and the guard arrived back
at the tunnel, Gordon was very rude.
"Pooh!" he said. "Edward can't pull the
train."

18

But they took no notice and Edward was coupled up behind the express. Edward puffed and pushed and pushed and puffed, but he couldn't move the heavy coaches.

"I told you so," said Gordon, rudely. "Why not let Henry try?"

"Yes, I will," said the Fat Controller.

"Henry, will you help to pull this train?" he asked.

"Oh yes!" said Henry, at once. "At last," he said to himself, "the Fat Controller *has* forgiven me."

So Gordon's driver and fireman lit Henry's fire. They broke down the wall and put back the rails. When Henry had built up steam, he puffed backwards out of the tunnel.

He was dirty and his boiler was black. He was covered in cobwebs. "Ooh! I'm so stiff. I'm so stiff," he groaned.

"Have a run to ease your joints and then find a turntable," said the Fat Controller, kindly.

When Henry came back he felt much better. Then they coupled him up at the front of Gordon's coaches.

"Peep, peep!" said Edward. "I'm ready!"

"Peep, peep, peep!" said Henry. "So am I!"

They started off. "Pull hard. We'll do it. Push hard. We'll do it," they puffed together.

Slowly the heavy coaches jerked and began to move. Then off they went, leaving Gordon alone in the siding. They went faster and faster. "We've done it together! We've done it together!" said Edward and Henry.

"You've done it, hurray! You've done it, hurray!" sang the coaches.

All the passengers were excited. The Fat Controller leaned out of the window to wave to Henry and Edward. But the train was going so fast that his hat blew off into a field where a goat ate it for tea!

The engines didn't stop until they came to
the station at the end of the line. All the
passengers climbed out and thanked Henry
and Edward.

The Fat Controller was very pleased. He
promised Henry a new coat of paint.

On their way home, Edward and Henry
helped Gordon back to the shed.

All three engines are now great friends.
Henry doesn't mind the rain any more. He
knows that the best way to keep his paint
looking nice is not to run into tunnels but to
ask his driver to rub him down when the
day's work is over.

THOMAS

EDWARD

GORDON